THE MAYOR IS MISSING!

by Tracey West

Based on
"THE POWERPUFF GIRLS,"
as created by Craig McCracken

SCHOLASTIC INC.

New York   Toronto   London   Auckland   Sydney
Mexico City   New Delhi   Hong Kong   Buenos Aires

ISBN 0-439-44223-0

Designed by Peter Koblish
Illustrated by The Thompson Bros.

12 11 10 9 8 7 6 5 4 3 2 1   3 4 5 6 7 8 /0

Printed in the U.S.A.

First printing, February 2003

The city of Townsville! Where the Mayor calls The Powerpuff Girls when the city needs help.

MAYOR

Brrrring! The hotline rang one day. But it was not the Mayor. It was Ms. Bellum.

"The Mayor is missing!" she cried.

The Girls flew right to City Hall.

"I cannot find the Mayor anywhere," Ms. Bellum told them. "Can you help me find him?"

"To find the Mayor, we need to think like the Mayor!" Blossom said. "What did the Mayor do today?"

Ms. Bellum gave the Girls a list.
The list showed all the things the
Mayor did that day.

Bubbles read the list.
"The Mayor went to dance class first," she said.

"Why would the Mayor go to dance class?" Blossom asked.

"We can ask the dance teacher," said Bubbles.

"The Mayor is our star dancer!" said the dance teacher. "He came for his class this morning. Then he left."

"To find the Mayor, we have to think like the Mayor," Blossom said. "Let's dance!"

After they danced, the Girls looked at the list.

"The Mayor went to the park next," Bubbles said.

The Girls flew to the park.

"Why would the Mayor go to the park?" Blossom said.

"The Mayor loves the park," said the park caretaker. "He comes here to ride on the merry-go-round."

"To find the Mayor, we have to think like the Mayor," Blossom said. "Let's ride!"

After the ride, the Girls looked at the list.
They went to every place the Mayor went.
They did everything the Mayor did.

MAYOR'S LIST

They played with puppies at the animal shelter.

They went to the movies.

They ate a big pizza with extra pickles.

The pizza place was the last stop on the list.

"After he ate, the Mayor said he was going back to City Hall," said the pizza man.

"What should we do now?" Bubbles and Buttercup asked.

"I guess we should go back to City Hall," Blossom said.

The Girls flew back to City Hall.
"We tried to think like the
Mayor," Blossom said. "But we
could not find him."

"It was fun being the Mayor," Bubbles said.

"Yeah," Buttercup said. "But it sure made me sleepy."

"If I were the Mayor, I would take a nap," Blossom said.

"Look!" said Buttercup. "The Mayor is taking a nap, too!"

"I guess thinking like the Mayor was the right thing to do!" Blossom said.

So once again the day — and the Mayor —
is saved, thanks to The Powerpuff Girls!